Disney PRINCESS

Beauty AND THE BEAST

Sleeping Beauty

Movie Theater Storybook
& Movie Projector®

Adapted by Rita Balducci
Illustrated by Disney Storybook Artists

CONTENTS

Reader's
Digest
Children's Books®

Pleasantville, New York • Montréal, Québec • Bath, United Kingdom

Beauty and the Beast

DISK I

I

In a small town in France, a long time ago, there lived a girl named Belle. She was smart and kind, and she dreamed of leaving her small town to have adventures like the ones she read about in books. Gaston, a vain hunter, hoped to make Belle his wife, but she was not the least bit interested in marrying him.

Belle was quite devoted to her father, an absentminded inventor. He understood Belle's dreams and wishes, and he loved her more than anything else in the world.

One evening, Belle's father became lost in the woods. He came upon an enormous castle and entered it. To his surprise, he found that the furniture inside

was enchanted.
He was even more
astonished when
a candlestick
named Lumiere
and a clock named
Cogsworth greeted
him and welcomed
him to the castle.

Suddenly, he
heard a fierce growl, and an enormous
beast appeared and cornered him.
"Please, I mean no harm!" Belle's father
begged, but the Beast took him prisoner.

2

When her father didn't come home,
Belle set out to search the forest where he
had gone. In time, she too came to the
Beast's enchanted castle. She found her

3 father locked in a dungeon in the castle.

"You must go right now!" her father
warned. But Belle would not leave and she
begged the Beast to let her take her father's
place as prisoner. The Beast agreed. There
was a spell over the castle, and the Beast
knew that if Belle came to love him, the
spell would be broken. Then he and the
enchanted furniture would return to their
original human forms.

Belle missed her father terribly, but she also found the castle to be a strange and wonderful place. The Beast told her she was free to wander throughout the castle, except for one room which she was forbidden to enter. One day, Belle's curiosity got the better of her and she decided to sneak into the forbidden room.

4 Inside, she found a rose under a bell jar, glittering and magical.

Just then the Beast bounded into the room. He was furious that Belle had disobeyed him. "What are you doing here?" he shouted angrily. Belle was terrified. She had never seen the Beast this angry.

Belle fled the castle and ran into the forest. A pack of hungry wolves chased her through the snow. As they were about to attack, the Beast appeared and chased them off, saving Belle's life.

Belle began to look at the Beast differently after he saved her. Soon they became good friends. Lumiere, Cogsworth, and the rest of their castle friends were very excited to see the change in the Beast. It seemed as though the spell was finally going to be broken!

One evening, the Beast decided to tell Belle that he loved her. They shared a romantic evening of dancing under the stars. "Are you happy, Belle?" he gently asked her. Belle told the Beast that she

would be happy if she could just see her father again.

With a heavy heart, the Beast said, "You are no longer my prisoner. Take this magical mirror to remember me."

6   Belle's father was overjoyed to see his daughter again. She told him how the Beast had changed, and of the many kind things he had done for her. A knock at the door interrupted them.

It was Gaston and a crowd of villagers. Belle's father had been telling tales about a strange beast, but no one had believed him. They all thought he was crazy and had come to take him to the insane asylum!

"I can help you and your father, Belle," Gaston said. "*If* you agree to marry me."

"Never!" cried Belle.

Gaston picked up the magical mirror and he saw a reflection of the Beast. "So this is who you care for?" he sneered. He turned to the villagers and shouted, "We must kill this wicked beast!" The angry

villagers followed Gaston into the forest, determined to kill the Beast.

Gaston soon found the Beast in the forbidden tower room. They fought on the slippery castle rooftop. Gaston drew a knife and stabbed the Beast. Suddenly, Gaston lost his footing and fell.

7

"Beast!" Belle cried, rushing to where he lay wounded. Tears fell from her eyes as she leaned forward, whispering, "I love you."

Slowly, the Beast rose into the air and began to change. Belle watched in astonishment as brilliant beams of light began to dance around him. As his cloak twisted and spun, the Beast was transformed into a handsome young man.

"Belle," he said, holding his hand out to her. Belle looked deeply into the young man's blue eyes. She suddenly realized that the handsome young man and the Beast were one and the same. "It's you!" she cried happily.

As the Beast was transformed, so were the rest of the people from his castle. Soon afterward, they all celebrated the wedding of Beauty and the Beast, and everyone lived happily ever after.

8

Sleeping Beauty

Once upon a time, there was a king named Stefan. When King Stefan's daughter, Aurora, was born, he invited everyone in the kingdom to join him in a great feast to celebrate the happy occasion. King Hubert and his young son, Phillip, were among the guests, for it had already been decided that Phillip and Aurora would marry someday.

Three good fairies named Flora, Fauna, and Merryweather were also invited, and they came with gifts for the child. Flora gave the baby the gift of beauty. Fauna gave the child the gift of song. Before Merryweather could give her gift, the evil fairy named Maleficent appeared.

DISK 1

She was angry she had not been invited to the party, so she put a curse on the baby. "Before the sun sets on her sixteenth birthday," Maleficent said, "she will prick her finger on the spindle of a spinning wheel . . . and die!"

Maleficent's power was so strong that neither Flora, Fauna, nor Merryweather could completely undo the curse. But because Merryweather had not yet given her gift, she was able to change the curse. Instead of dying, the princess would fall asleep and remain that way until she received a kiss from her true love.

To protect Aurora, the fairies took her to a cottage in the woods where they lovingly raised her. So no one would know who she was, the fairies changed her name to Briar Rose.

Briar Rose grew up not knowing she was a princess, but she was beautiful and good. On her sixteenth birthday, the fairies sent her out to pick berries so they could make her a special dress. Briar Rose happily obeyed her dear friends.

As Briar Rose walked through the woods, she began to sing a love song. Her voice was so beautiful that all the woodland animals gathered to listen.

A young man on horseback heard the singing, too, and he rode toward the sweet-sounding voice. He was enchanted by Briar Rose's song and he began to sing along with her. At first, she was startled to see the young man and hear his strong voice joining with her own. He seemed like a prince out of one of her dreams. She was captivated by the young man.

They danced together as they sang, and by the end of the duet, the two young people had fallen deeply in love.

When Briar Rose arrived back at the cottage, she breathlessly told the fairies that she had fallen in love with a young man in the woods. It was then that the fairies had to tell her the truth about her birth and her name. She was heartbroken to learn that she was truly a princess, and was already betrothed to Prince Phillip. With a heavy heart, Aurora walked with the fairies back to her father's castle.

Aurora was home at last, but her mind was on her true love. Suddenly, a strange green light caught her eye. She followed

the light all the way to the tallest tower in
the castle, where a spinning wheel glowed
in the corner. The fairies realized Aurora
was in danger, and they raced to stop
her from touching the spinning wheel. But
before they could stop her, Aurora pricked
her finger on the spindle. She instantly fell
to the floor and lay motionless.

The fairies laid Aurora gently on her bed.
"The king and queen will be heartbroken,"
they said. "To save them from this
heartache, we must put everyone else in
the kingdom to sleep."

3

At the very same time, the young man with whom Aurora had fallen in love came to the cottage looking for her. Instead he met the evil Maleficent. Maleficent knew the young man was really Prince Phillip, and she quickly chained him in her dungeon.

The good fairies soon discovered his true identity and came to his rescue. They freed the prince and gave him a magic sword and shield to fight Maleficent. Prince Phillip slashed his

way through the brambles surrounding the castle. Maleficent turned herself into a huge dragon and set fire to the brambles.

Prince Phillip bravely fought the dragon, using his sword to kill the evil creature. Then he raced to Aurora's side and kissed her. The spell was broken! Aurora's eyes opened to see the face of the young man she loved, and all over the kingdom, everyone else awoke, too. The fairies were overjoyed as the happy pair joined hands. True love had conquered all!